Larry Silva

The Warri‹

MW01140270

Great Legends of the Forest I

Larry (Chas) Silva

Warrior Publishing

Edited by Dona Sturmanis Mfa

Book Design by Rand Zacharias

Cover Artwork by Scyap Design Team

Library and Archives Canada Cataloguing in Publication

Silva, Larry
     The Warrior and the Wolf

ISBN-13: 978-1505281729

ISBN-10: 1505281725

Larry Silva

Dedication

This story is inspired by my mother and father who through their teachings made me the man I am today.

PREFACE

When the earth was young and the waves of the great ocean swept onto the land, the First Nations people were created. As the world changed and life evolved, freedom could be found wherever these people ventured and they were born to thrive within it.

Their world was a place where everyone lived as one with nature. The people respected the land, the water and the animals as these provided the necessities of life like shelter, food and clothing and many other things needed for their survival.

Eventually, the people became divided into different groups called clans or tribes. Some of the tribes moved inland to live in the great valley while others chose to build their settlements along the coast near the ocean.

The seemingly never-ending valley was surrounded by majestic mountains covered with trees as old as the earth itself and the animals that dwelled there were plentiful.

The clans believed that some of these animals were the tribal elders who had passed on and again became one with nature so they could remain living in the valley and watch over the people. They also believed that the old chiefs who died became part of the wind that blew across the ocean so the spirits of these great leaders could protect Mother Earth. It was also believed that the warriors who died in battle and couldn't sing their songs of death were taken by the Great Spirit and turned into stars so the people could look at them at night and always remember them.

Each tribe was led spiritually by a shaman or holy man. These men were special and revered by all, as it was said these seers could look into the future or the past.

These holy men would tell the people of the Great Spirit that sometimes came to earth and took the form of a black stallion with four white hooves. It was told he would run amongst the human beings and when he returned to the sky, he would fly towards the sun and the wind flowing off of his back would create the rainbow.

The shamans believed that if you followed the rainbow to its end, there you would find heaven and the Creator.

There are many stories amongst all native tribes of how things came to be and this is a story of perhaps the greatest warrior who ever lived....

CHAPTER ONE
A Warrior is Born to the World

The year was 1532 when the child was born into the world. He was the son of Shesa, his mother and Black Eagle, who was the chief and a mighty warrior of the great Wolf Clan. This child would one day become a great leader like his father and grandfather before him.

On the day of his birth, his father held him up to the sky and said, "Behold my son, Great Spirit, for together we will teach him to become a mighty warrior and protector of his people."

It was the right of Shesa, his mother, to name the child, so she called him Nikotay, which meant Prince of the Forest. As the boy grew, he would come to share a great bond with a white wolf, a native princess he would grow to love and with all the human beings of the great valley.

It was winter season throughout the land, a time of hardships, of heavy snows and hungry villages. There were five clans living in the valley with enough land for each to live and hunt and to flourish as a people. The Wolf Clan controlled the centre of the valley. The Beaver Clan lived to the north across the great river; to the south was the Eagle Clan, to the east the Fox Clan and west towards the ocean was the Great Bear clan.

The Bear Clan was led by a mighty but ruthless chief who thought that all tribes of the valley should become one again, with him as the leader. His name was Two Crows, a great warrior in his own right. The other clans feared him, but the Wolf Clan was strong and as long as Black Eagle was alive, the villages would remain separate and at peace.

Black Eagle was a great man and a wise leader—he was quite striking, with a muscular body and piercing eyes as well as long, black hair flowing down his back like the mane of a stallion. He stood six-foot-two, which was tall for the people of that time, and weighed in at about 200 pounds. Black Eagle was highly respected by all living in the valley and along the coast; even the enemies of his people knew him as a great warrior.

The Wolf Clan stayed within their own territory as did most of the clans, and respected the agreement the grandfathers had made to keep peace. However, there were those who were greedy and wanted all the land....
Each clan knew that entering another's territory uninvited to cause trouble could mean war or some show of strength to keep the land from being taken. However, if a chief rode into another's camp unarmed and in peace, he was welcome. Even though this was agreed upon and understood by all, occasional raiding still went on.

Every few years, the different clan leaders would meet to talk of the future of the people, the great valley and to air any grievances they might have against another tribe. Some of the talk was about Two Crows pressuring the other leaders to join him, but the chiefs always refused.

The meetings were held on neutral ground in the sacred caves hidden behind a giant waterfall cascading down the mountainside into a huge crystal blue pool. The people always felt that the pool was created by rain falling from heaven itself and was ever replenished by the great river's waterfall. The caves had been around since the beginning of time and were known only to the shaman or chief of each clan, so in case of war, the villages that wanted peace could hide safely. The caves were like a fortress and easy to defend.

Life in the native villages was mostly peaceful and serene. Each clan had its own chief and elders who taught the people how to survive and what was expected of them. The camps were usually set up in a big clearing surrounded by many tall trees to slow the wind that blew into the valley from the ocean. These camps would be built near a river so there was always a clean water source close by. Even though there were many day- to-day hardships, everyone was happy and secure.

Life was much the same in all of the villages of the valley as well as within the camps of the coastal tribes. The elders cleansed themselves in the sweat lodges while warriors stood guard around the camp protecting everyone as they had been trained to do since they were young men. The children ran around laughing and playing without a care in the world while their parents went about the daily chores of the village. Other children sat in a large circle around the old ones, listening intently to the many stories of what they were and where they came from. The old ones were well looked after and highly respected as their teachings and stories held the secrets to the past and future of the people. Other youngsters who were a little older helped out as everyone in the village young or old contributed in some way.

The women had important roles within the clans. Without their hard work and dedication, life in the villages would have been much more difficult. It was the job of the young maidens to collect wood and to keep the fires burning. Other girls were out in the forest collecting berries, roots and other foods so no one would go hungry. Girls reaching maturity would sit with their mothers and the older women to learn to sew animal hides to make moccasins and other clothing to keep the clan warm in the winter months and to learn the duties of a wife and mother. Other women would clean fish for smoking or bake bannock in crudely-made ovens, while others would repair the tepees that had holes worn in them and let in rain. All the women were talking, laughing and singing as the children played around them and tried to learn the songs they were hearing and what they meant.

The men and boys had tasks to perform as well. As they grew, the young braves would play warrior games to sharpen their skills for when they were older and would take their places as the hunters and protectors of the clans. Nikotay always excelled at these games and was a little stronger and faster than the other boys. Competition amongst them was always friendly, as even among children, unity was the way to strength within the tribe. They were taught from a young age that a warrior who stood alone was never as strong as many who stood together.

The older warriors taught the braves who were coming of age the things that were taught to them like how to make tomahawks or which trees would produce the best bows. They taught the braves how to make other weapons like knives out of bone or antler and arrowheads out of stone. While they did this, they would tell the young men of the great hunts and the many chases of the great herd of wild horses that ran free in the forest and mountain passes.

The herd was led by a mighty grey stallion, with four white hooves, that seemed like he could never be caught. They called this stallion Mesa, which meant the grey ghost, because as he ran, he seemed to vanish into the landscape. Nikotay always bragged that one day, the grey stallion would be his. This herd of mountain horses had been around since the days of the grandfathers' grandfathers and had become legend. All the boys would listen in awe to the stories and daydream about when they were older and could ride alongside the great warriors and go on the chases of these amazing animals.

But for now, there was much to learn. There were daily practices of shooting bows and arrows and how to throw knives and tomahawks for close-in fighting. These teachings were passed down from warrior to warrior and father to son for generations. They were also taught to track an animal without being seen or heard. They also learned how to skin it and use every part of the animal as nothing went to waste.

These very important lessons prepared these young ones for the day when each boy turned 16 and had to endure their rite of passage to becoming men.

The older warriors showed the young braves how to carve totems to mark the life journey of the tribe. These totems would stand tall and forever for future generations to see—it was important for the children and the grandchildren to know of the past and how their ancestors lived.

Fish were an important part of the people's diet, and although women knew how to fish, it was the task of the young men to put makeshift nets across the river to catch trout and salmon.

In the late summer months, the salmon would leave the protection of the ocean and make the great journey up the river to spawn and lay their eggs to create new life. The shamans said the souls of the dead mother salmon would call to their young to get them to swim upstream from the ocean. Salmon were very important to the people of the valley as they provided food in the winter months when game was scarce.

Salmon were also very important to the coastal tribes, but they had a different method of catching them and other fish as they were the people of the ocean. The men made longboats out of giant trees that would carry many warriors. They also made spears and the women would make nets. They would paddle these longboats a short ways out on the ocean and would hang the nets over the side; the fish would swim into them and become trapped.

When the nets were full, they would haul in the salmon and fill the boats. Sometimes a hungry seal would follow the nets and when it got close enough, they would spear it. Seals went a long ways in feeding a village.

The ocean tribes also ate clams and oysters and other crustaceans that were found on the beaches. Like the valley clans, they also hunted for game in the forest.

Often Nikotay and Black Eagle went to the river to fish. His father would tell him many tales of what it took to become a warrior. Black Eagle spoke of his own adventures as a young brave and how he would ride alone into the mountains to go after the grey colt born into the great herd that ran free there. They would talk for hours and the young brave learned many things on these trips. Black Eagle taught only his son the secrets taught to him by his own father who was once chief and had passed the leadership torch to him. He said he who carried the sacred staff of a hundred generations was recognized as leader. He taught Nikotay that a clan chief had many responsibilities to his people and didn't eat or sleep until everyone in the village had a full stomach and a warm place to sleep. Nikotay looked at his father and idolized him as he was a great man.

As the son of a chief, Nikotay was loved by many and his parents and grandparents were very special to him. He learned many things from them and they spent much time together. From his mother, Shesa, and grandmother, Penat, he learned patience, truth and strength of character. From his father, Black Eagle, and grandfather, Natosa, he learned how to survive, but mostly what it takes to be a leader of men.

Nikotay's grandfather would always say that he had made the boy's father a chief and one day it would be his grandson's turn to lead. He told Nikotay many stories of his mother and father and of the history of the valley. Grandfather spoke of the great wars of the past when the warriors of the northern and southern coastal villages would send their war parties to raid in the great valley. Many times they attacked and were fought off by the mighty warriors of his grandfather's village.

The great valley was of one clan then, with Nikotay's grandfather as leader. They had many braves and always stood strong together against all enemies. The coastal tribes finally asked for peace as they were losing too many men and would soon have few warriors left to protect their own camps. Some of the elders of the valley didn't want peace and inner dissension among the people started to manifest. Eventually they left to start their own clans in different areas of the great valley and along the coast.

Nikotay's grandfather told stories his own father had told him about evil spirits that sometimes came from the ocean and took the form of men. They traveled in giant canoes and sometimes took people with them as they headed back out to sea. These lost souls were never seen again. When the old chiefs died and were taken by the wind, they would travel across the ocean to search for these lost souls. He wanted his grandson to know that evil comes in many forms.

One day when he and the old man were out walking in the forest, Grandfather Natosa turned to him and said, "I have something for you, my grandson." He handed him a drum that he had made from deer hide and a medicine pouch containing a bright blue stone. He told Nikotay the stone was special—it had been blessed by the Great Spirit and carried many powers including the power to heal. The old man said that when he was a young boy, he found the stone while swimming in the sacred pool at the bottom of the waterfall and thought that it must have been put there by the Great Spirit so the people would know that it was a sacred place. It was said the blue stone had the power to catch the rays of the sun and reflect light into the cave so the people could see in the darkness. Natosa told Nikotay the drum was special also and could communicate with the Great Spirit himself. His grandfather told him if he ever needed him he could bang the drum and he would always hear it. He hugged Nikotay—and the boy was happy for the gifts and carried them with him wherever he went.

His grandfather was getting older now and his face and body were showing the wrinkles and scars of many battles before peace came to the valley. One day when Nikotay was about 10, the old man was out walking in the forest and went missing. Day after day, clan members searched for him but without success. The story goes that the old one was close to death and had made his way to the ocean, where the Great Spirit heard the old chief's death song and sent the wind to take him.

The boy partially accepted this as truth, but his grandmother did not—she always said that her husband would never leave the earth without taking her with him. Nikotay never told the villagers the story his grandfather had told him of the evil spirits that sometimes came from the ocean. He thought they would be happier thinking the missing went into the forest to be alone while they sang their death song to the Great Spirit and had their souls returned to nature. His father once told him a wise chief had many secrets. And sometimes it was better to keep things to himself for the good of the people.

Nikotay missed his grandfather and he felt bad for the elderly woman who was now without her husband. The boy and his grandmother would often ride to the shores of the great ocean where they would light a fire and sit there while Nikotay played the drum. His grandmother would hold the blue stone in her hand while she sang, hoping the old man would hear her and be happy in death knowing she was thinking of him.

Nikotay's grandfather had been a great man and his grandmother was a great woman and he loved them dearly. He helped his parents to care for his grandmother the best he could until her own death a few years later. She would always claim the old man was still alive and had been taken by evil spirits, but they thought these were just the ramblings of a distraught old woman and ignored them.

The boy returned to the ocean many times after her death. He would stand at the edge of the great water and call out to the evil spirits that might have taken his grandfather:

"I am Nikotay, son of Black Eagle and Shesa of the great Wolf Clan and one day I will become a mighty warrior and lead many braves. When I was born, I was blessed by the Great Spirit. Return my grandfather, or when I die and become one with the wind, I will fly across the ocean and kill you—then you will be no more...."

CHAPTER TWO
Meeting Tihla

As time went on and Nikotay grew older, the young brave accepted all challenges to prove himself to his mother and father and the rest of the village.

It was summer in the valley and life in the camp was going on as usual. Black Eagle and a few warriors were at the waterfall meeting with the other leaders. The people were tending to their daily tasks as the sun shone brightly over the mountains. Warriors stood guard around the encampment and other men shot arrows from the backs of their horses at makeshift targets as small boys mimicked them. Children played and Nikotay could smell venison cooking on an open fire. His mother and some other women from his village were at the river bathing and washing clothes and he could hear them talking and laughing. He thought to himself that life was good and he was happy.

Nikotay was 13 now and for fun, he would often run through the forest as fast as he could. As he ran, he would sometimes see a pack of wolves shadowing him with a huge white wolf in the lead. However, he was well armed and wasn't afraid. Sometimes he would see the white wolf alone, and as he ran, she would run parallel to him. He would laugh and call to her, "Run with me, for we are both mighty creatures of the forest and I am your friend." Sometimes, the white wolf would run close to Nikotay without ever attacking and just as quickly disappear into the cover of the forest.

His mother told him the wolf was the spirit of his grandmother watching over him and was running through the forest still searching for her husband. Sometimes, when Nikotay would ride to the ocean to play the drum for his grandfather, he would see the wolf on the beach, howling to the waves as if they were alive and expecting them to answer back. Nikotay would stand at the edge of the water, and while the wolf howled, he would stare out at the ocean. As the crashing waves were trying to make themselves part of his thoughts, he would think of his grandparents and daydream of becoming a man. In the back of his mind, he could hear his father telling him, "Be patient, my son, as the ways of a warrior and leader take many years to learn."

In the spring and summer months, the people were preparing for the coming of the salmon. Game in the forest was plentiful and many times the hunting parties went out. Moose and elk were the main diet of the village and were always dangerous to bring down. The older warriors would go after these great animals while the younger braves would go after smaller game like rabbits, grouse and small deer as they were taught to do. Occasionally, a few braves wanted to become warriors before their time and would try to bring down a moose, elk or bear and often at the loss of their lives. It didn't happen often as the fathers would forbid their sons from doing this.

Nikotay was a leader among the young braves and would often think about proving himself as the future chief by bringing down one of these huge animals on his own. He would also think of riding into the mountains and capturing the grey stallion that he had heard about for most of his life and his father had chased as a young boy.

All of the braves wanted to do the same as this elusive animal that ran like the wind was on the minds of all warriors of each clan. Even the coastal tribes to the north and south would follow along the ocean to the great valley where they would pass through on the way to the mountain passes to go after the great herd. They came in peace and were unmolested as they rode through. Even in their villages, it was said that the white footed stallion was an offspring of the great black spirit horse that travelled on the rainbow and good luck would come to whoever might catch it. Many times, the warriors of the great valley chased the herd in hopes of claiming the grey for themselves but all tribes, whether inland or coastal, were never successful as this horse was smart and knew the trails and mountain passes as well or better than most, as he had run them since he was a young colt. All the native people were great riders and had been on horses since they could walk, but Nikotay knew if he hoped to capture the grey, it would have to wait until he was older.

One day, some of the warriors of the tribe led by Black Eagle were going after the wild horses and Nikotay and a few others who were coming of age got to go along. The warriors were mounted on mighty steeds adorned with many colours on their backs and huge feathers and claws hanging from their manes and tails. They had captured these horses from the herd on previous hunts and they could run quickly enough to keep up to the wild horses they were after.

As they rode through the forest towards the trails leading to the mountain passes, the young braves said to each other that today they would become men and capture the grey stallion. Nikotay said nothing. He would watch his father and do as he did. The older warriors would laugh amongst themselves listening to the young braves. Still, they were proud as the young men were growing strong and talking without fear. As they rode along, they would teach the young men what signs to look for when trailing the wild herd and how old some signs might be. It took more than just following hoof prints as the herd would cross their own tracks to throw off their potential captors or predators that would stalk them like grizzlies, wolves or big mountain cats.

Further up the mountain trail, the horse-hunting party came upon the carcass of a huge cat that had been trampled. They knew it must have been the grey leader as this 250 pound predator was no match for a 1200 pound stallion protecting its fold. These big cats would go after the younger horses and colts but were often denied as the young were well protected.

The giant grizzlies were a different story because of their immense power. These great beasts were huge, standing nine feet tall and weighing in at 1800 pounds. The herd would rely on their sense of smell and amazing speed to avoid these dangerous animals.

Wolves were smaller and slower and had trouble chasing down the herd. They preferred to hunt deer and smaller game in the cover of the forest where they were much more successful.

As the warriors reached their destination and rode into a clearing, they saw the horses on the other side of the meadow feeding on the mountain grasses and enjoying their freedom. The herd consisted of 20 mares, five younger males and two young colts, all of which were offspring of the grey. The stallion was nowhere to be seen but the hunters knew he wasn't far away.

Suddenly, the great animal burst into the clearing and reared up on his hind legs to warn the intruders. This was the first time that the young braves saw the grey and they were in awe and afraid at the same time. They quickly gave up any thoughts of trying to capture this huge animal—he was a magnificent stallion and bigger than life as he stood tall with the mountains behind him. As he came down on all fours, he called to the other horses and off they ran. His speed was amazing and the warriors gave chase with Black Eagle in the lead.

Nikotay remembered the stories his father told him as a younger boy of the many chases such as this. The young braves had trouble keeping up but it was all part of the training. As the chase went on, the other horses of the herd followed the grey stallion every step and were losing the warriors. Suddenly, the trail they were on split into two and the herd stayed on the path that went to the left along the cliff, hoping to lose their potential captors. These warriors, however, were experienced horsemen and never missed a step. The chief told some of the men to go to the right and they would meet up at the end where the two paths came together—hopefully one of the two groups would get ahead of the herd.

A new chase was on and as they neared the end of the trail, Black Eagle saw the other group had gotten ahead and was trying to block the path. The grey stallion didn't slow at all and he and the herd ran through them like they weren't even there. As they ran by, the warriors were able to throw ropes on four mares.

The prize was the grey stallion, however, and Black Eagle really wanted him. The mare that ran closest to the stallion was his mate. She was all white and her colt wore the colour of his father. The warriors wanted this colt also but every time they got close, the grey stallion would intercede running into their horses and knocking them over.

The warriors ended the chase as their mounts were tiring, but were happy with the captured mares. They saw the grey stallion a quarter mile up the mountain standing on a bluff looking down on them. He shook his head up and down and snorted as if laughing at them. Then he called to his captured mares and they answered back. Black Eagle gazed up at him and said, "Next time, my brother," but he had said that many times before. Then he looked at his son and smiled.
Nikotay smiled back, then looked up at the grey stallion and whispered to himself, "One day, great horse...one day."

As the warriors rode back to the village led by their chief, the young braves were excited but realized their thoughts of catching the grey at their age were impossible. Still, their hearts were full of pride for being a part of this great chase.

When they reached the camp, everyone ran out to see the new additions to the herd. There was much excitement and many stories would be told of the hunt—the legend of the grey stallion would grow. They knew tonight there would be dancing and celebration to thank the Great Spirit for the good luck on the hunt and the safe return of the braves. There would be a feast—the women would prepare special foods and the warriors would tell stories of the bravery of the young men.

There were always many dances and celebrations in the village to show gratitude as this was part of the native way of life. The clan would celebrate a bountiful harvest or the coming of the salmon. The warriors would dance around a huge fire to get ready for war and would ask the Great Spirit to bless them. There were dances when two people joined in marriage or to welcome the coming of a new leader. These dances were meant to bring the people together as one with the Great Spirit which was their greatest strength. Tonight, the people feasted and the fires burned brightly in the darkness of the night and the villagers were happy.

It would be another year before Nikotay would go through his rite of passage. He was growing ever impatient. Even though he knew it was forbidden, he had talked some of the boys into going with him on a hunt for one of the larger, more dangerous animals found in the forest. They thought it would be a good test for any young warrior reaching manhood.

He told them to gather their weapons and they would meet at the edge of the clearing that surrounded the camp.

They were to tell no one, and even though they were afraid, the young warriors tried not to show it and set out on the hunt. They saw many tracks and knew which ones to look for.

Nikotay and the other braves were on the trail of a huge elk when they noticed wolf tracks crossing the trail in front of them. He recognized these tracks as belonging to the wolf that often shadowed him, and was sometimes seen on the outskirts of the village standing just within the tree line.

As they were of the Wolf Clan, the young braves took the wolf tracks as a good sign. They were closing in on the elk and knew if they could kill this great animal it would feed the village for at least a month and possibly ease the trouble they would be in when their fathers found out what they were doing.

Nikotay saw that the elk tracks led out into a clearing and the braves followed quietly. The other boys hung back a little as they wanted to avoid startling the animal. It was mating season and a 1300 pound male elk with huge antlers that stood six feet at the shoulder was dangerous and something to be feared.

As they stepped quietly out of the cover of the forest into the clearing, Nikotay saw Tihla for the first time. He could tell she was of the Beaver Clan from the way she was dressed as were the warriors standing guard. She and the other maidens were gathering wood for the fires of their village—Nikotay could see she was a beautiful young girl and he couldn't seem to look away. Her father was

Pantos, the chief of her tribe, and her mother, Mehote, was a beautiful woman also. Yet, there was something familiar about this girl, Tihla, like he had dreamt about her all his life but had never met her. She looked up at him but didn't run, and as he stared into her innocent brown eyes, they touched his soul like the first time he saw the sacred pool at the waterfall. She was breathtaking and he couldn't help smiling at her—and she smiled back. She was about 13 and just becoming a young woman; he was 15 and was on his way to becoming the great warrior his father was. Still, they were old enough to know the ways of the old ones and unless one was a chief, direct contact with other clans was not permitted.

They looked at each other for what seemed like forever, but it was only a moment. As the young braves turned to leave and return to the forest, Nikotay heard the loud crack of a tree giving way to a force greater than itself. He heard a wolf howl in the distance and he took it as a warning to be on the alert for danger. He had heard these howls before, like when a raiding party was making its way through the valley, or when grizzlies were on the hunt for prey and near the camp.

Suddenly, the great elk appeared into the clearing. This animal was huge and its eyes were red and swollen. As it snorted, steam streamed from its nostrils. The elk bellowed loudly, then lowered its head while swaying its huge antlers back and forth. It stamped at the ground with its hooves and charged towards the young Beaver maiden. Tihla tried to move, but she seemed frozen in place, so she closed her eyes to prepare herself for the inevitable goring she was about to take....

Nikotay was already reacting and released two arrows into the majestic animal before the other warriors started to attack. The elk was hit twice more and was badly injured but still it wasn't stopping. Nikotay pulled his knife and put himself between Tihla and the huge animal. The elk came down hard on him like a tree falling from a mighty wind and tried to gore the young brave. However, Nikotay was quick, moved to the side and leapt onto the animal's back. He stabbed the great elk repeatedly but was quickly thrown to the ground as it continued its assault.

The elk sunk its antlers into his shoulder, and the injured brave gasped as he lay there with the elk standing over him. He saw one of his own braves moving in to attack and the animal was temporarily distracted. Nikotay knew he had only one chance and he reached up and plunged his knife deep into its heart, ending the attack and the great animal's life.

The other boys pulled the elk off of him as the braves of the Beaver Clan rushed the frightened maidens into the forest. Tihla stopped for a moment to look back and smiled at him again as if to say thank you for saving her life before she faded away into the cover of the trees. Nikotay quickly bandaged his injured shoulder and approached the dead animal.

He felt bad for killing his brother elk but the stomachs of his people would now be full and their hunger tempered. The young braves were excited and hollered to the sky as their fathers had done after such a successful hunt. While they cut the elk into pieces to bring back to the village, Nikotay cut out the heart of the great animal and held it up to the heavens as an offering. He had seen his own father do this many times and felt pride as he said loudly, "Thank you, Great Spirit, for the gift of food. I offer you the heart of my brother so you may return him back to nature." He then dug a hole in the earth and buried the heart.

While they finished skinning the great animal, two boys built a travois to transport the carcass. The young warriors were proud of what they had done and walked along with their heads held high.

As they were heading back, Nikotay caught a glimpse of the wolf. He called to it and said, "Thank you, Grandmother, for the warning." The wolf stopped for a moment to look at him and then vanished into the forest.

When the young men returned to the village, the chief, Black Eagle, was angry, but that quickly subsided when he saw that all were safe. The people were already splitting the meat into shares for each family and everyone was excited and talking of the kill. There would be no celebration for this hunt as the young braves went against their fathers' wishes, but they had shown they were well on their way to becoming capable young men.

Nikotay's wounds would heal, but the young brave had proven he was a warrior in the body of a boy and could help to look after his people. He would always remember that moment with the elk, and when he would look at the scars from the attack, he couldn't help but think of the young native girl and wonder about the strange feelings coming over him.

CHAPTER THREE
The Rite of Passage

As another spring turned to summer, it was a special time for the Wolf Clan. It was now 1548 and the day had come when Nikotay would turn 16 and he and three other young braves would go through their rite of passage into manhood. Nikotay was a leader among the younger men, but today each boy was on his own. If the braves made it through, they would become young warriors with more rights like the older warriors had. They wouldn't quite be adults yet, but they wouldn't be looked on as young boys anymore. The ones who failed would have to wait one year before they could try again. Each boy usually passed this test of maturity as their fathers had readied them for this day since they were born.

The ritual was extremely difficult and dangerous—each boy would go into the forest without food or water or weapons to protect them. They were to walk on separate paths towards the sacred waterfall where the shaman would be waiting. Once there, they were to sit by the water without talking. The holy man would be above them at the top of the waterfall chanting to call for the Great Spirit. They were not to eat or drink along the way, or the spirit horse would not appear to the ones who did not respect the laws of the ritual.

After two full days without eating or drinking, they would have a vision and the black spirit horse would appear to each one. The spirit would take human form and whisper to each brave a secret word known only to them and the shaman of their clan. If on the third day, the young braves survived the fasting and had not been killed by wild animals, they would head back to the village and go to the tepee of the shaman who had returned the night before. He would ask each brave for his secret word.

It was said the holy men of each clan were seers and knew things no one else did. It was told they could see into the future, and through their dreams, they could enter the world of life or death.

While the Wolf Clan shaman meditated and chanted at the waterfall, the Great Spirit would enter his mind and tell him the secret words. If on the third day a brave did not return, or said the wrong word, the holy man would know his vision was false and the brave would be denied the rite of passage.

Knowing this, the young braves set out into the forest but they felt uneasy about what was to come. They had known each other since they were born and had become friends. They had heard many times of the braves who did not return. Some were never seen again; others were killed by wild animals and the tribe later found their mauled bodies in the forest with tracks surrounding them.

Before the braves separated to walk their own paths, Nikotay told them not to worry and to be strong. He reminded them of their elk hunt a year earlier and how they had achieved a great thing. They nodded their heads and laughed nervously, but were still somewhat afraid. Nikotay told them Black Eagle said that fear makes a man sharper and more aware, and if they used it, they would certainly succeed and return as warriors. And with that, they went their separate ways.

It was a warm spring day in the great valley. The trees were being blanketed by fresh leaves and growing flowers were adding colour and mystery to the tall grasses of the meadows. Nikotay heard the sound of a doe calling her fawn and the birds chirping as if warning each other of movement in the forest. These sounds had always put Nikotay at ease, and he thought to himself it was a good day to become a man. As he walked, he couldn't help thinking of the grey stallion and how he had avoided being captured throughout the years. He thought about his father, of Tihla, and of the great chase he and the other young braves had been on with the warriors and how exciting it had been.

As he moved through the forest, he felt he was being followed and would catch glimpses of movement from time to time. He decided he would hide behind a stump just off the path and wait for whatever was following to come out in the open.

Then it appeared—the white wolf. Nikotay stepped out from his hiding spot. When the wolf saw the brave, she stopped and looked at him. Nikotay spoke to her and said, "Hello, Grandmother, today I will become a young warrior and ask for your blessing."

The white wolf never took her eyes off him—then she ran towards one of the trails that led to the mountain passes. Nikotay watched her vanish into the forest. Suddenly, he saw movement further up the trail where the hill crested and assumed it was the wolf again. He turned to head towards the waterfall and took a last look back.

There, standing at the top of the hill, were the grey stallion and the white mare. Nikotay thought it was strange they were alone as the herd never ventured far from the leader. He was excited by what he saw, but he knew he had to go on.

He called to the grey stallion and said, "Today I am becoming a man, but I will see you again, mighty stallion." Then he made his way towards the path that followed the river as it was the shortest route to his destination. In the distance he heard a noise like the cry of an injured animal. He stopped walking to listen closer and heard it again. It was the cry of a foal—he knew something was wrong, and he couldn't just leave it to the predators that would surely find it.

Nikotay needed a closer look but how would he do that without being killed by the grey or its mate? As he walked up the hill towards the sound he heard, the stallion moved forward. It shook its head and stamped its front feet as if warning Nikotay to stay back.

The young brave moved slowly towards the grey and talked to it in a calm voice, saying, "Do not fear, my brother. I am here to help you." He was trembling slightly as he kept moving forward. The stallion calmed down as if it understood the young brave meant them no harm.

When Nikotay got near the top of the hill, he spotted the young foal laying on the ground just off the path. It was less than four months old and was the exact colour of its father.   Its leg was injured and bleeding and Nikotay could tell from the gaping wound, it had been made by the claws of a grizzly. The foal couldn't walk and was panicking as the brave approached it.

The grey stallion and mare backed up slightly to allow the boy access to the young horse. Nikotay talked quietly to it as he had done with the grey. He looked into its eyes and said, "Be still, little one. I am Nikotay and I am not here to hurt you."

As he whispered to the little colt to ease its anxiety, he picked up some clean leaves that had fallen to the forest floor and began to clean its wound the best he could. He looked at its mother—she was acting nervous and running in circles. The grey wasn't within view and the brave felt uneasy. Nikotay stepped away from the colt for a moment to look around for the stallion so he would be ready to move in case he was attacked.

What he saw made the hair on the back of his neck stand up. Less than 50 feet away, a 1600 pound grizzly was coming out of the brush and it was hungry. The bear was looking for the colt that it had injured and was following its scent right to where it lay.

The mighty grey stallion confronted the grizzly and put itself in front of the huge animal and reared up. The bear stood up and came towards the stallion with its claws ready to strike. As the grey came down, it lashed out with its front legs and hit the vicious animal on the side of the head with its hooves, knocking it over.

The bear was stunned for a moment, but was unhurt. It again stood up and as the horse was rearing up again, the bear slammed it with a mighty paw and the grey went down. As it lay catching his breath, the grey was mostly unharmed. He called to his mare and she ran off.

While this great battle was going on, Nikotay had gotten the colt to its feet and was already halfway down the hill. He helped it to walk and half carried it towards the river. The bear saw them and wanted the easy prey, so it gave them chase. The brave saw it coming and when he and the colt were almost to the river, he noticed there was a big log jam on the shore that had been deposited there after the winter thaw when the river was at its highest. If he could reach it, he and the colt might have a chance.

Nikotay turned to look at the pursuing grizzly who was almost upon them. He and the wounded colt made it to the river; he climbed under the logs and pulled the wounded colt as far under as he could. The bear's power was incredible as it was tearing the logs apart like they were dried twigs. He was growling loudly and reaching for them with his four-inch claws and massive teeth. It wouldn't be long before he got to them.

All of a sudden, the stallion appeared and was again trying to protect its foal. It turned its back end to the bear, and as the mighty grizzly turned to again face it, the grey kicked out with its back legs and hit the bear cleanly. The grizzly was knocked onto its back and was stunned.

Nikotay knew this was their chance and crawled out from under the log boom as quickly as he could, pulling the injured foal with him. The grizzly was again up and ready to attack and Nikotay knew it was only a matter of time before the bear killed one or both of them.

Suddenly, he heard a familiar howl and the white wolf ran out of the forest, putting itself between Nikotay and the great beast. The bear tried to get around the wolf, but she stayed in front of it matching the hungry animal move for move. The wolf snarled ferociously, baring its huge canines, and the great bear swung its mighty claws at the wolf, which if connected, would surely kill her with one swat. However, she was fast and avoided being struck.

As the wolf kept the massive bear busy, it gave Nikotay time to lift the injured colt onto the back of its father and also climb on. He knew he wouldn't be thrown off as the stallion would not throw its own offspring. He grabbed the mane of the great horse and hung on, holding the colt as they rode off.

Even with the extra weight, the stallion's speed and strength were amazing. It seemed to take Nikotay's directions even though it was the first time that a human was ever on its back. Suddenly, the herd of horses ran out of the forest, led by the white mare and joined them on their run. The bear was on its feet and giving chase, but they got a head start and were losing the big grizzly as he faded out of sight. Nikotay looked for his grandmother wolf but she was nowhere to be seen. Yet again, she had helped to save his life.

The herd headed for the mountain pass and once there, Nikotay jumped from the stallion's back, took the colt down and laid him on a bed of branches that had fallen from the trees. The adult horses were not aggressive towards the boy as they seemed to sense his good intentions. He built a fire near the wounded horse to warm it and as the sun went down over the valley, he nestled in beside it and fell asleep.

As night turned to morning, Nikotay noticed the colt hadn't moved much. The animal had lost a lot of blood and its wound was festering from infection. The boy tried to use leaves and damp moss to clean the wound, but he didn't have the skills of a medicine woman. She knew which herbs to use to make a poultice and the chants needed bring the spirits to take away the sickness.

Nikotay sat with the little horse throughout the day and talked quietly to it to try to somewhat ease its pain, but without the poultice, the colt had little chance. His worried mother walked around them, sniffed the air and trotted off. From time to time, the grey would look over and the brave saw the stallion was on edge but had no injuries from the grizzly attack.

As he sat there, Nikotay thought of his friends at the waterfall and wondered what they must be thinking of his absence. Maybe they thought he was dead as no boy missed his rite of passage. It didn't matter, though—to him, saving the young horse was more important. It was the second day since the attack and the colt seemed worse. He knew it was just a matter of time and he felt sadness at his inability to help.

Again, he lit a fire to keep the colt warm in the cold night, and he looked into its eyes. The colt looked back and Nikotay could tell it was in a lot of pain. If on the third day the colt was still not doing well, he would end its life to ease its suffering.

The grey still commanded the herd and would approach from time to time. Nikotay would walk up to it and put his hands on its neck; it would look at its offspring and in its eyes, the brave saw the wisdom of many years of life.

As Nikotay sat by the fire and the sky summoned the moon, he heard the howl of a wolf in the valley below. He smiled as he knew it must be the howl of his grandmother telling him she was all right. He was tired and he thought of his parents as laid down beside the fire and drifted off to sleep beside the colt.

As he slept, he dreamt of the black spirit horse. He was on its back as it flew over the great valley. They passed over the village and he saw the wolf pack running through the forest. He saw the young braves heading back from the waterfall and the shaman sitting at the fire near his tepee while he chanted.

Nikotay awoke and immediately checked on the colt. It wasn't doing well and he knew the time had come. He looked at its mother and father and picked up a rock to hit it as it had suffered enough. Before he struck it, he looked to the mountain as if asking the Great Spirit for forgiveness. He saw the vision of the black horse, and from where he stood, he could see the rainbow at the waterfall. He thought about what he was about to do and lifted the rock over his head.

Just then, the colt raised itself slightly and looked into Nikotay's eyes as if to say it understood. It put its head back down and the brave hesitated for a moment, then threw the rock to the ground. He called to the grey and he and his mare approached. He tried to speak to the stallion with his mind and the grey lifted its head up and down as if understanding.

He picked up the dying colt and again the stallion allowed Nikotay to put the colt onto its huge back. The grey looked at the boy and didn't move, so again the brave jumped on, held onto its mane, and off they ran with the white mare following close behind.

They raced for the village and as they rode in, everyone ran towards them as they had thought Nikotay was dead. Everyone shouted with amazement as the son of their chief was riding atop the greatest horse that ever ran in the valley. His parents came out of their tepee where they had been since his disappearance. His mother was crying and his father couldn't believe his eyes, but was happy to see his son.

Nikotay rode past them and straight to the tepee of the medicine woman. She approached and told him to bring the dying colt inside. He left the young horse with her and she immediately made a poultice and applied it to the wounded leg. She then started smudging the animal while she circled him and began to chant.

He walked outside to the grey and his mare and led them to the corral where they kept the other horses. As they entered, they were immediately recognized and surrounded by the other horses, and were at ease. He looked into the grey's eyes and whispered, "Everything will be okay."

He then approached his mother and father and as he hugged his mother, Black Eagle put his hand on Nikotay's shoulder and said, "Welcome back, my son. To see you makes my heart glad."

All day long, the people surrounded the corral to see the stallion and there was much excitement in the village. No one talked of Nikotay's rite of passage and he didn't care as it would wait until next year.

The other boys had returned and were now young warriors. Nikotay thought only of the colt as its future wasn't promising. As he waited for a sign from the medicine woman, he walked with his father to the corral, and the grey stallion and the white mare would approach him as if asking about the colt. His father was amazed by the grey stallion's reaction to his son. As he went to touch the animal himself, it moved away. He would then put his hands on top of Nikotay's and feel the stallion's power through his son's hands as he touched the grey.

After two days, the medicine woman appeared from her tepee and the brave feared the worst. Then, from the opening of her tepee, the young horse stuck out its tiny head.

Nikotay smiled and was happy, and the stallion reared up in the pen and whinnied to his son. The mare ran around in circles and then stood beside her mate. The colt came out but was limping, and when the people went to surround it, Black Eagle stopped them as the stallion began to snort and act up.

Nikotay led the colt to its parents and the young horse leaned on its mother. The young brave began feeding the other horses and the colt approached him. He held food out to the colt: it ate while Nikotay hugged its wobbly frame.

Over the next few days, the colt grew stronger and would often follow Nikotay around the camp. He grew to love the horse and wanted to keep it. He would take the grey from the pen, and with a makeshift bridle, lead it around and the colt would follow.

After many days, the young foal was just fine and as Black Eagle and his son walked together with the stallion his father asked him what he would do with the horses as they were now his. Nikotay handed him the bridle and said, "The grey will be yours, my father, and the white mare will be my mother's, but I would like to keep the colt."

The chief was happy as he had always wanted this awesome stallion. He thanked his son and told him to return the stallion and colt to the pen. The boy obeyed and as he closed the gate, the stallion approached him. Nikotay rubbed his neck and said, "Do not fear, mighty horse, for you are among friends." As he walked away, day was turning to night, and while the village slept, all was quiet.

Nikotay awoke the next morning and his father asked his son to walk along the river with him.

"Freedom is important," Black Eagle said as they strode along. "All people and creatures deserve to be free and are happier that way."

Nikotay nodded his head. He understood what his father was trying to say.

"A man makes many hard decisions that affect his life, and this one will affect yours," Black Eagle said to his son.

As they walked back, Nikotay told his father in great detail of the grizzly attack and how the wolf had again protected him. Black Eagle was proud and told him a chief and leader was always ready to sacrifice his life for others.

When father and son reached the camp, everyone followed them to the corral to see what would happen. Nikotay opened the gate and said to the grey stallion, "I release you and your family, my brother." He hugged the colt. Off ran the grey stallion, the white mare and their offspring towards the forest.

The boy lowered his head and walked towards the tepee of his mother and father to be alone. He heard a noise in the bushes and out ran the grey colt. The young horse approached him, and as the stallion and mare watched from the forest, it ran into the corral and stood there.

Black Eagle laughed and said, "It looks like we have a new member of the village." As Nikotay hugged the colt, the grey stallion and his mare had long disappeared into the forest and back to the herd.

For rescuing the colt from the grizzly, and his relationship with the wild grey stallion, his father and the elders agreed Nikotay had earned his rite of passage. The young warrior was happy, and as the years went on, the colt grew into a great stallion. This horse loved to run and had the speed of his father. When he galloped all out, his eyes seemed to shine brightly so Nikotay named him Chasa, which meant "eyes of fire."

Nikotay and Chasa would ride through the forest as fast as they could, with the white wolf giving chase. Sometimes they would ride into the mountain passes so the stallion could see his mother and father. Nikotay would sit down to rest and release Chasa to join the herd and off they ran together. As he sat on the mountain, he would think of many things and Tihla, the girl he loved, was always first on his mind. The young stallion loved the young warrior prince, and after spending time with the other horses, would always return to him.

CHAPTER FOUR
The River

It had been four years since the grizzly attack and Nikotay was 20 years old now—a full-fledged warrior of the Wolf Clan. One day, he said to the other warriors of his tribe that they should go on a raid of another village as he wanted to test himself against the men of the other clans. He asked his father if he could take 50 braves and go on a raid of the coastal villages, but his father would never allow it. He was a wise chief and had always told his son that peace was the way to the survival of his kind, and a great chief thought of his people first.

So Nikotay would settle for running far into the forest and goading the warriors of other clans into chasing him. He would run away laughing with the white wolf trailing him. The warriors tried hard to catch him, but he was too quick and agile and they were always unsuccessful.

Stories were soon told in villages of a great young warrior who ran with a white wolf and had tamed the grey stallion....the legend of Nikotay was growing.

Sometimes he would ride his horse to the edge of the river and would see Tihla on the other side. She had become even more beautiful since the first time he saw her. She and the other maidens were washing clothes, bathing or swimming, but always under the watchful eye of a few warriors standing guard. These women knew they were never to be out in the forest on their own without protection.

Sometimes Tihla would see Nikotay watching her and would look back at him as if to say, I remember you. She thought he was very handsome, with his muscular body and long flowing black hair, sitting proudly atop his grey stallion.

He was maturing and the females of his tribe were drawn to him. They were beginning to wonder which one of them he would choose as a wife. He never showed much interest. He often wished that the clans could communicate more with each other so he could talk to Tihla and tell her of his feelings. But going against his father's wishes could mean death, even for him.

One time, Nikotay was out riding and saw Tihla swimming in the river. He stopped to watch her for a moment before moving on, and he noticed she got out too far and the current started to sweep her away. She swam as hard as she could but the current was strong and carried her a long ways downstream. The protecting warriors chased after her as did Nikotay, but the river was fast and she was soon out of sight.

When Tihla was able to reach the shore further downstream, she found herself on the wrong side of the river. She was afraid and knew that the only way back to the safe crossing to her village was through the forest. She stayed hidden as much as she could as she made her way back upstream. She hoped she would soon run into her own warriors that she knew were looking for her.

As she walked, she heard voices and the pounding of many hooves in the distance. When they got close, she crawled under some bushes and peaked out slowly. Tihla saw warriors with bear claws hanging from the manes of their horses. She knew it was a raiding party of the Bear Clan and she was in danger of being taken or killed.

The Bear Clan warriors were fierce and mighty-looking. She kept very still. Tihla didn't know it at the time, but they had also seen her in the river and were looking for her.   They were closing in, and as they rode by, one of them spotted her and called out to the others. She jumped up and started to run, but knew she wouldn't get far. She heard the sound of footsteps behind her, and as she turned to see who it was, she tripped and fell. A mean-looking warrior was just about to jump on her and she closed her eyes and braced herself.

After a few seconds nothing happened. Tihla slowly opened her eyes and the enemy was lying beside her with an arrow in his chest—he was dead. She thought her own braves had done this, but when they didn't appear to her, she knew she was mistaken.

Two more warriors appeared from the forest and when they saw one of their own braves lying dead, they pulled their knives and moved towards her. Tihla covered her face and peeked out between her fingers.

Suddenly Nikotay came out from nowhere confronting the intruders. He waved his tomahawk menacingly and said loudly, "I am Nikotay, son of Black Eagle of the great Wolf Clan and you do not come in peace. Leave our land or die."

The enemy warriors looked at each other and one of them attacked him. While they rolled on the ground, another one moved towards them, knife in hand. As he raised his knife to strike, the white wolf suddenly appeared from the forest and jumped on the intruder, knocking him to the ground.

As she stood over him, she put her huge fangs close to the warrior's face and looked into his eyes. The man dropped his knife and didn't move. The wolf growled deeply and then ran off. By this time, Nikotay had overpowered and wounded the other brave. He stood them up with a knife to the throat of the wounded man and told them how lucky they were to be alive. He let them go and they both ran off thinking the Wolf Clan's power was much stronger than they were expecting.

Nikotay then heard the sound of horses and saw his fellow tribesmen chasing after the raiding party and running them back to their own territory. He carried the dead warrior's body to the water and put him in so he would float down the river and back to his people near the ocean as a warning that raiding in Wolf Clan territory was not a good idea.

He approached Tihla and helped her up. She looked deep into his eyes and then noticed the scar on his shoulder from the attack of the elk many years ago. She had heard the stories of the warrior who ran with the wolf and had thought about him over the years. She leaned forward and hugged Nikotay as she trusted him and was not afraid.

He called for his stallion and the horse came running. Nikotay climbed on his back and pulled Tihla up behind him. She put her arms around him and as they rode to the crossing, they talked of the attack that just happened and she said the Bear Clan often made their way into Beaver territory. Two Crows would ride into the camp accompanied by many warriors and talk to her father about joining him and becoming one clan. Her father always refused, but with so many warriors against him, he knew he stood little chance. Two Crows wanted the braves of her village to join him so he would be as strong as the Wolf Clan and he could take over the valley. He would ride into their village in peace and leave in hostility.

Tihla told Nikotay some of the people of her village had disappeared and a short time ago, her mother went missing as well. Her father was never the same since that time and she felt he was giving up. He searched for his wife for many days, but he never did find her. It reminded Nikotay of his missing grandfather....

Two Crows would often ask Tihla to come back to his village with him and become his wife. She always said no. Then he would tell her that one day, he would be the leader of all the land and take her as his own. Two Crows and his braves would then ride away with a thunderous roar of pounding hooves....

When Nikotay and Tihla reached the river crossing, they saw her father Pantos and a few warriors from her village just on the other side. They were looking for her and she called to them to let them know she was safe.

Pantos smiled with joy that his daughter was okay. Then she ran to him over the safe crossing of the river.

She told her father what happened and how a warrior and a wolf had protected her. The Beaver chief somewhat doubted her story, but when he looked across the river, he saw Nikotay galloping away on his grey stallion, followed by a white wolf.

Tihla's father recognized him as the Wolf Clan prince and yelled out to Nikotay, thanking him for saving his daughter. He wasn't sure if he was heard, but it didn't matter because Tihla was safe and that was the important thing.

Nikotay stopped for a moment to look back. He held up his hand to say goodbye to the Beaver princess, then rode away and hoped he would soon see her again.

He met up with the other warriors of his tribe who were now making their way back to the village. They told him they had heard the sound of horses in the forest and rode by to investigate. When they saw what was happening, they chased the intruders back to their own territory, and while laughing, said it would be a while before they would see them again. They rode back to the village with their heads high and with a pride only a warrior feels when he has defeated his enemy and protected his village.

As they rode into camp, Nikotay's father had already heard from a scout of the encounter with the raiding party. He approached his son to see for himself that he was all right and was proud of him. His mother appeared from her tepee and ran to Nikotay. He climbed off his horse and hugged her, then turned to his father and said, "Today, my father, I have fought in battle and defeated the enemy of my people."

Nikotay never told Black Eagle about Tihla, only that he had run into a raiding party and chased them off after killing one man. He told his father the brave attacked him and taking his life was the only way to defend himself. Then, secretly, he told his mother about the girl as he needed to speak to someone of his feelings. His mother told him she already knew, as a woman and mother knows these things. Shesa never told her husband what she suspected.

She said to him that when he became the leader, he could try and change the minds of the elders and be with her; it would take time. "The future of the valley is in your hands," said his mother.

Tihla was often in Nikotay's dreams, riding her horse on the other side of the river and always in the same direction he was riding. She would call to him and then disappear. Even though it was only a dream, he knew that he loved her and one day they would be together....

CHAPTER FIVE
Evil Comes

As the year progressed, there was little trouble in the valley. One day, Nikotay was entering his father's tepee, and inside, there was a meeting of the elders in progress. He sat to listen, but could say nothing and heard that again, Two Crows was pressuring the other clan leaders to join him. Soon the leaders of each tribe would meet at the waterfall and this and the raids would be discussed again.

Something had to be done about Two Crows. Nikotay wanted to be at his father's side for the meeting as he felt his father might be in danger while leaving the safety of his territory. Black Eagle was himself a great warrior and told his son not to worry. He always knew that Two Crows wanted control of the valley, and as long as the native leaders stood strong together he could do nothing. Still, Nikotay was worried, so his father agreed that his son was a man now and deserved to be there.

On the way to the meeting with his braves, Nikotay told them to spread out and be ready for anything. They were well-trained and very courageous, and as they rode the trail they had ridden a thousand times before, the white wolf was never far from sight.

When they made it to the waterfall, everyone was there except for the Bear Clan chief. While they waited for him to arrive, the other clan leaders talked amongst themselves and complained of the pressure Two Crows was putting on them to join him. Although they were against it, they felt like it was only a matter of time before he would attack them.

Two Crows had told each leader that the medicine of the Bear Clan was powerful and evil spirits would come from the ocean to help him in taking the land and the people. Only the Bear Clan would be left standing unless they agreed to join him.

Nikotay wondered why Two Crows was not killed when so many stood against him, but it was not his place to speak out unless asked. His father had told him before that killing each other was not the answer unless absolutely needed. He had said to Nikotay that sometimes evil spirits entered the hearts of the people and made them them do things they wouldn't ordinarily do. He had known Two Crows as a young boy and they were once friends, but something had turned him towards evil. He was hoping his old friend might change back as no one in the history of the First Nations people was born with evil in their hearts.

The other leaders at the meeting turned to Nikotay and addressed him. They said they had heard of a strong young brave who rode a grey stallion, ran with a wolf and had attacked the Bear Clan raiding party. Pantos spoke up and told the others that Nikotay had protected his daughter as well and had killed one of the Bear Clan braves.

"I am only here to protect my father," said Nikotay. "As the leader of his people, Black Eagle will speak for his village." He did, however, feel pride for the acknowledgement from these great leaders.

After hearing the Beaver Clan chief's story, Nikotay's father looked at his son and suddenly realized why he was never interested in the advances of his own village women. He had heard of the beauty of the Beaver Clan maiden, and being in love with a special woman himself, he understood what his son wanted, but could do nothing about it. The laws of his ancestors had been in place for many years and no one had ever gone against them.

Just then, a few of the Wolf Clan braves entered the cave and said a scout had told them of strange-looking human beings in the forest. They were being led by Two Crows and many warriors and were still a ways away but were heading in the direction of the caves. Two Crows had waited for the tribal leaders to meet at the waterfall and after taking over their villages, he could find them in one place and kill them all.

Black Eagle told his scouts to trail the war party that was coming and they left. He then told his son to take the braves and go warn all the different villages that there were strangers in the land; evil was coming. He said to bring all the people to the sacred caves where they would be safe and protected.

Each chief gave Nikotay something they were wearing that told the story of their people so each village would believe the words of his warning and follow him. His father told him that his spirit was with him and while he was gone, he and the other chiefs would make plans for an attack of their own.

Nikotay and his warriors raced off to the Fox and
Eagle Clan villages, told them of the events that were
unfolding and that they should flee for the caves. They
knew who he was and when he showed them the items
their chiefs had given him to prove his word was real, they
knew he spoke the truth.

Their own scouts had heard many horses in the
forest, but disregarded it as they thought no one would
dare cause trouble on this sacred meeting day. The
villagers quickly headed towards the waterfall, led by a
Wolf brave, while Nikotay and the other warriors moved
on to the Beaver Clan village.

He went as quickly as he could, but when he got
there it was too late. The people were gone except for a
few dead braves. He looked around and noticed the tracks
of the missing were leading to the ocean.

Suddenly, a group of people came out of the forest
where they had been hiding. Nikotay asked what
happened and they said that strange beings wearing clothes
that shone like the sun had suddenly come into the village
without warning and had gathered the people together,
killing some of them. He looked for Tihla and they told
him she had already been taken.

Many other tracks were heading to the waterfall, so
Nikotay knew that the strangers and Bear Clan warriors
were heading that way. Again, he had a few of his braves
hurry the people to the caves. He needed to get to his own
village to warn them and he was worried for his mother.

When he arrived at his own village, it was also empty, so he gathered his warriors and they headed for the caves. On the way, he ran into some of his people being led towards the waterfall by his mother and he was happy she was safe.

His mother told him the white wolf had entered the village and begun howling. She knew by this that something was wrong and told the people to go into woods. Just then, they were attacked and only half the village got away. The rest were rounded up and taken towards the ocean. She described the attackers as odd-looking humans who spoke gibberish and were vicious in their assault. She said the captured were taken away by a few braves and they took them towards the ocean while the rest of the attackers headed towards the waterfall.

Nikotay told his mother to lead the people back to the sacred caves before the enemy got there and he would catch up. Then he told her of a secret trail his father had told him about that would get them there ahead of the war party. He said he wanted to go to the ocean and see his enemy up close.

When he got there, he hid up on a small cliff overlooking the beach. As he looked down, he saw an odd sight. The evil spirits were very strange-looking as his mother had described and their giant canoes even stranger. There were two canoes as large as the biggest long houses, and they stood as high as the tallest totem. The strangers were shorter than the human beings and their skin was shiny in the sunlight.

Nikotay thought they must be talking the language of the spirits as he understood nothing of what they said. There were about 300 evil spirits there as well as many Bear Clan braves standing guard. They were bringing the people onto the canoes and whipping them when they moved too slowly. Tilha was nowhere to be seen and he thought maybe she was already dead. He knew it was time to get back to his father.

On his stallion, he caught up quickly with his mother and the others who were now entering the caves as well as the members of the Beaver and other clans who were also arriving.

He told his father and the other chiefs the news of their villages and what he had seen at the ocean. They counted about a hundred human beings who were missing, but still 700 people had made it to safety.

The chief of the Beaver Clan looked for his daughter but she wasn't here. Nikotay didn't say whether or not he had seen her at the ocean as the distraught chief was already unhappy enough about his wife who had vanished some months earlier.

When Nikotay's father saw Shesa, he held her for a moment and then looked towards his son who he knew was thinking of Tihla. The Wolf scouts who were trailing the war party came back and said the enemy was getting close. The warriors heading to the waterfall consisted of the Bear chief and 50 braves. With them were a hundred evil spirits who looked like men and carried magic sticks that sounded like thunder across the sky. They also carried strange boxes that Nikotay thought must be filled with magic or the souls of the captured.

Everyone started to panic and the elders said they had no chance. How could they stand against evil spirits and so many mighty braves? Tihla's father was worried for his daughter and knew he had little chance of ever seeing her again.

Black Eagle tried to reassure them that it would be all right, but they did not believe him as they were afraid. They wanted to leave the great valley and go into the mountains to hide.

Everyone was talking at the same time and suddenly a loud voice shouted out above the rest. "People of the great valley, hear me. I am Nikotay and I am a mighty warrior of the Wolf Clan. The Great Spirit lives within me and I am not afraid. On this sacred ground, I will fight forever those who try to take away my land and my people. Stand strong with me and I will lead you."

Black Eagle knew right then that his son was now ready to lead the people, so he let his son continue speaking.

Nikotay told the people that the enemy was expecting to fight small groups of warriors from each clan and not all the clans' braves together fighting as one. They were 350 warriors strong and could stand up against any enemy, even evil spirits that came from the ocean to take them.

He told 50 braves to go above the great waterfall and gather rocks to throw down on the enemy. He told another 200 braves to split up and hide in the forest on each side of the waterfall to attack the enemy from behind when they were entering the caves and least expected it. The 100 remaining warriors would attack from the front when the enemy was distracted by the ambush from above and to the sides. He said their enemy would stand no chance and would be overpowered before they knew what hit them. Then, they would ride to the ocean to save the captured people. He told them not to attack until he gave the word. All of the leaders from each tribe agreed including his father.

The enemy finally arrived and approached the waterfall. Moving in slowly, they stopped at the water and Two Crows called out to the villagers, "Come out, people of the valley, and join me. I will lead you and you will not be harmed." The people didn't trust him and Two Crows had no idea of the ambush that awaited him.

The leader of the strangers was getting impatient and yelled loudly the words of his language. He spoke directly to Two Crows who translated the words. "People of the forest, come out and be captured, or we will send in thunder boxes that will destroy the caves and you will all die." The people were afraid when they saw that the Bear chief understood the words of the evil one and thought his soul must have already been taken.

The enemy heard a howl in the distance and looked up. There at the top of the waterfall stood Nikotay and at his side was the white wolf. Two Crows knew this wolf as the one he heard about in the past from his raiding party and knew the Wolf brave's power was strong.

Nikotay stood tall and said, "I speak to you as a protector of all the people. Leave this land and go back to the ocean where you came from or you will all die."

The enemy should have heeded this warning, but didn't, and they all moved towards the caves. Nikotay yelled out, "Be ready, my brothers and sisters, for on this sacred ground walks evil, and together we will stand strong against it."

The men leading the attackers through the waterfall to the entrance of the caves were quickly overtaken by the waiting warriors from inside and killed. When the ones following behind saw them fall, they backed out a little, and were suddenly hit by giant rocks raining down on them. They panicked.

The villagers started hearing the thunder of the evil ones and were frightened. Nikotay yelled, "Attack, my brothers!" and suddenly, the warriors hiding at the sides of the waterfall attacked and the enemy started to fall. They fought back as best they could, but were overwhelmed. The ambush happened so quickly that the enemy had little chance to use their weapons. A few of them managed to get away, including the leader of the evil ones, as well as Two Crows, and a few of his warriors who were now running into the forest and back towards the ocean.

When the remaining enemy turned to face their attackers, the hundred braves inside the cave attacked and again took their backs. They stood no chance but the evil ones' thunder sticks were powerful. They pointed these sticks at people and they fell dead. Nikotay thought they must be spirits because they possessed a great magic. However, he was confident the magic of his people was stronger.

They lost 30 braves to the enemies' powerful weapons but had protected the sacred ground and those inside the caves. Everyone hoped the bigger fight that was waiting for them at the ocean would turn out much the same, but the element of surprise was now gone.

Nikotay knew they had little chance and he and the other chiefs talked of what could be done. They decided to take the elders and the people, accompanied by 20 braves, into the mountains to hide because the enemy now knew their location. He told his father he and the 300 remaining warriors would get to the coast as quickly as possible. He hoped they could catch up to Two Crows and the evil spirit leader before they reached the ocean and warn the others of the attack that was coming from the human beings. He hugged his mother and father and told them he loved them.

They rode as quickly as they could but never did catch up to the attackers. On the way, they heard the howling of the wolf as if guiding them and took it as a good sign.

Nikotay and his braves reached the cliffs of the ocean and saw many people on the beach below. The evil spirit chief was telling his men to load the human beings onto the canoes as fast as they could. Nikotay was afraid for the captured people as well as his own warriors. He noticed many of the captured were not from the valley but from the coastal villages as well.

Just then, Tihla appeared on the beach being dragged by Two Crows. Worried she was being handled by the Bear Clan chief, Nikotay was still hugely relieved she was alive. However, he knew all the people were in grave danger. He knew the giant boats would be leaving soon, but how could he get near them without being discovered?

Tihla was resisting and Two Crows said to her, "Look at your people being taken away by the evil spirits. The same will happen to you as I had done to your mother if you don't agree to be mine."

She looked at him and realized he was the one who took her mother. He wanted to trade her mother back to her people for Tihla, but didn't get a chance as the evil spirits took her from him. She started to cry for her mother.

Two Crows noticed that some of his own men were being disarmed and loaded on the boats as well. When he approached the evil leader to find out why his own men were being taken, the evil leader told him to tell his braves to drop their weapons and to get all of his people on the boats. Two Crows called to his warriors to attack and when he turned, the evil leader pulled out a long, shiny knife and stabbed him. The chief fell, badly injured.

The evil one grabbed Tihla and told his men to take her aboard. When they saw their chief fall, the Bear Clan warriors started to attack, but the evil leader was ready and his men had many magic sticks. The thunder roared loudly, and many warriors fell, but now all of the warriors of the Bear Clan were alerted and joined in the attack.

Nikotay saw the men on the boats open the magic boxes and take out round objects. They then put these balls in long tubes that protruded from the sides of the boats. The evil one told his men to put fire to them and after a loud noise was heard, many of the villagers fell dead at the same time. They did this many times and many people died. The people stopped attacking and turned to run. Most were quickly surrounded and again, started to be loaded on the huge boats.

When the remaining warriors were being rounded up, Nikotay thought this was their chance. He told his men that 50 warriors, including himself, would slip down to the beach and pretend they were with the captured people and let themselves be taken on the boats. They would hide knives and tomahawks in their clothing, and when he signaled, the remaining Wolf Clan warriors were to rush the boats and attack. Fifty braves would stay on the cliffs shooting flaming arrows down on the evil ones, as Nikotay thought that fire might cleanse the evil spirits of their human forms and send them back to from where they came.

Once aboard with the other braves, he would try to somehow free all the captives. To signal his men, he would loudly bang his drum.

The evil ones didn't notice Nikotay and the other braves slipping in amongst the prisoners. They were all loaded aboard—after all, to them all native people looked alike.

Once aboard, Nikotay noticed the people were being put into cages. Some recognized him. He told them not to speak and they understood that a plan was in place. A few of the now imprisoned Wolf warriors whispered to the people of each cell to be ready and passed out a few of their small weapons to as many as they could. They also handed some weapons to villagers from the coastal tribes as they were all in this together.

When the captured were all secure, most of the evil ones went above with only a few left standing guard. The leader was still on the beach with most of his men as they were guarding the beach from attack by the warriors that he thought were coming while his men finished loading up. He told his men to make the boats ready so they could sail away before the attack.

One of the evil guards was talking to the captives, but they did not understand his words as only the evil leader spoke some of the language of the human beings. He went above and brought back with him a man who walked as though he was very old and somewhat crippled. He had a hood on that covered most of his head. Nikotay could only see a part of the old one's face, but couldn't make out who he was.

This hooded man somehow spoke the language of the people and translated the words of the guard. He said, "Be still and be quiet or we will point our magic sticks at you, and when you are dead, we will throw you into the ocean. Then your souls will forever be trapped in the deep waters."

The hooded man had trouble walking from the many beatings he must have endured as a captive of these cruel spirits. Nikotay thought he must have been a mighty warrior at one time because of the way he spoke to the people and because it seemed his soul hadn't yet been taken from his body. He wondered who this man was and where he might have come from.

From another cage, breaking the silence of his thoughts, came a familiar voice calling out to him. It was Tihla and she was speaking to him just as she had done many times in his dreams. She was afraid and he told her not to worry.

He felt it was time for action before the giant canoes left the beach and he told the people to start making as much noise as they could. The guards told the hooded man to tell everyone to quiet down, and they began to whip some of them through the bars. The braves who were armed grabbed the guards who got within reach and pulled them over to where they could put knives to their throats.

They weren't sure how to open the cages but the hooded man knew. Before the other captors could react, he grabbed shiny things from the guards being held and put them in the doors of the cages. Magically, they opened. The other guards whipped the hooded man and he fell to the floor. It was, however, too late as the warriors were now free. They overtook all the evil spirits guarding them and quickly killed them.

Nikotay went over and helped the hooded man to his feet, and thanked him for helping to set them free. Without removing his hood, the man told the Wolf prince he was taken years earlier and had been kept alive to translate the evil words of his captor to any human beings who were ever taken prisoner. The old man was injured and seemed close to death. Nikotay wanted to see who this brave man was, and when he removed the hood, he gasped.

Before him stood his grandfather, who was much older now. Nikotay was so glad to see him—the brave warrior hugged his grandfather and the old man said tearfully, "My grandson, I have missed you and now see that you've become a mighty warrior."

Nikotay smiled and then turned to Tihla and pulled her to him. They hugged for a moment and he looked deep into her eyes. Then he asked her to look after his grandfather.

The now-freed warriors let out a mighty yell as they followed the Wolf prince out of the belly of the canoe and into the sunlight to attack.

The evil leader heard the commotion and ordered his men back on board. As they started to run from the beach towards the boats, the leader heard a familiar howl. He and his men stopped to look up to the cliffs. Above was the white wolf and many warriors. Suddenly, fire came from the sky. Many spirits fell, and as the leader turned towards the ocean, he saw that the villagers were free and attacking his men on the boat. He ordered the second boat to fire their cannons at the cliffs and the remaining soldiers would help the first boat.

Just then, he heard the war cries behind him coming towards the beach. Nikotay banged the drum loudly and yelled to the 200 warriors to attack quickly as he thought the second boat would never fire thunder at their own spirits that were now among the attacking warriors on the beach.

The evil leader would prove them wrong and he climbed aboard the second boat. He told his men to fire cannons onto the beach and many on both sides were killed.

Nikotay remembered the battle at the sacred pool and guessed that while in the form of men, the evil ones could be injured or killed. He wanted to save his people before these evil men changed back into their spirit forms.

The first boat was overtaken and he noticed Tihla and his grandfather were again captured. They were being taken aboard the second boat, and it started to sail away towards deeper water. Some warriors tried to swim out and climb aboard, but it was too late.

Just then, they heard loud war cries coming from the ocean. Many coastal warriors were now arriving in longboats and began attacking the second ship. They had come to rescue their own people and had heard the drumming and understood it. They knew it was coming from the Wolf prince, as they had heard it many times at the ocean over the years.

Nikotay and his men swam out while the warriors on the cliffs continued shooting flaming arrows into the giant canoes. The evil leader told his men to keep shooting their cannons at the beach and into the water to repel the attack, but it was failing. Tihla protected the injured old man as best she could. She told him she was of the Beaver Clan and when he heard this, he told her an older Beaver woman was on board the second boat and was locked in one of the cabins. She guessed it must be Mehote, her mother.

By this time, Nikotay and his warriors were climbing aboard as were the warriors from the longboats. There were so many braves attacking.

Tihla ran to Nikotay and said, "My mother is aboard and is locked somewhere inside." He told some warriors to watch her and his grandfather while he found Tihla's mother and set her free.

The warriors grabbed Tihla and the old man and jumped into the ocean to swim back to shore.

The Wolf brave found Tihla's mother very quickly and brought her on deck—she jumped overboard and started swimming to the beach. Nikotay saw the giant canoe had many small fires on it. Many arrows had hit the magic boxes that were on board, setting them ablaze. He knew giant thunder was coming to the boat and would soon destroy it. Almost all the evil spirits were now dead except for the evil spirit leader and a few wounded.

This leader was ruthless and powerful—Nikotay grabbed him and put a knife to his throat, but didn't kill him. The captives on the second ship were already being freed and were jumping into the ocean and swimming for the beach. Nikotay ordered everyone including the other tribes' warriors to get off the boat and they obeyed. He released the leader and jumped into the ocean, leaving the evil spirit on board the burning ship. He knew the leader would stay on board and not dare swim to the beach as he would be killed instantly.

The evil leader yelled out loudly to the human beings in his spirit language. Then there was a huge blast and the giant canoes slowly disappeared below the ocean waves.

Tihla cried and hugged her mother while people stood over his grandfather, who was laying on the beach and dying. Nikotay ran to his side and leaned over the old warrior. He knew it wouldn't be long.

"You are still a great warrior and have helped to save your people once again," he said to his grandfather. He played the drum and sang for his grandfather, and the old chief smiled. Just then, the white wolf approached and Nikotay saw she was badly injured. She laid down beside the old man and howled at the ocean for the last time before she died.

Nikotay hugged the wolf and thanked his grandmother for being his friend and protecting him on so many occasions. He reached into his medicine bag and took out the blue stone and handed it to his grandfather. It had protected him in life and maybe it would protect the old man in death while he searched for the lost souls. The old man told Nikotay that he loved him and was proud of him. His grandfather placed the blue stone on the back of the dead wolf and then passed away.

CHAPTER SIX
New Life

The people on the beach were sad and started to sing the song of death for the old chief so his soul would rise and become part of the great wind. As they did this, the spirit of Nikotay's grandfather rose from his lifeless body and floated out just above the waves. This spirit looked like his grandfather, but as a young warrior again. His spirit cried out towards the heavens and a great light shone from the sky. The blue stone started to glow. All of a sudden, the spirit of the wolf rose from the body of the animal and turned back into his grandmother, but as a young Indian maiden.

Their souls had always been as one and could not be separated in life or death. As the wind started to take them away, Nikotay's grandfather spoke to the people and said, "Behold all of my native brothers and sisters of the earth, if we stand strong together as one, no evil can ever defeat us. Be strong, my grandson, as my spirit will always be with you." Then the spirits of his grandmother and grandfather slowly turned towards the ocean and disappeared onto the wind.

Nikotay gathered his people together, including the chiefs and warriors of the coastal and Bear clan. He wanted the other villages of the coast to join all the people of the great valley at the sacred waterfall. He believed as the new leader of the Wolf tribe that all the human beings of the world should have a voice about what happened in their land, whether they were coastal or inland First Nations people.

As they started to leave, Nikotay heard a faint voice calling from down the beach. It was Two Crows—he was badly injured and barely alive. As the people surrounded the once great warrior, he started to speak: "My brothers and sisters, I ask for your forgiveness for what I have done. An evil spirit entered my body and showed me greed. It never reached my heart as I have always loved my people." Everyone believed him as all knew that greed was never the way of a First Nations warrior.

Two Crows turned to the Bear Clan villagers and said, "Be well, my people, for you are all now one with the great Wolf Clan." Two Crows looked to the sky and said, "Great Spirit, please release my soul from the evil spirits that inhabit my body, as I was once a mighty warrior and great leader of my people. But most importantly, I was a good man." Then he closed his eyes and life left his body.

Nikotay touched his forehead with the blue stone that he had retrieved from the beach and said, "Great warrior of the First Nations people, we forgive you and your spirit will stand as one with us forever. Our children and grandchildren will tell stories of your greatness and not of the evil forced upon you. Greed is not our way, but forgiveness is."

He put the blue stone back into his medicine bag and told his warriors to put the Bear chief's body onto a horse to take back with them, as well as their fallen brothers and sisters. Then they all made their way to the waterfall.

He sent warriors ahead to tell the people they were on their way and to come down from the mountains and meet them at the sacred caves. Once they arrived, his parents were waiting and were so happy to see him. He told them what happened at the ocean and about his grandparents. He said they were finally together again and died happy.

Tihla's father saw his wife and daughter and they ran to him. He hugged them both and was glad they were alive and well.

The people of each tribe surrounded the waterfall, and together began singing the song of life and death as Nikotay carried the body of Two Crows into the sacred blue pool.

"Sacred water and giver of life," he began, "I offer to you the body of a once mighty warrior. Cleanse his soul and take him with you back to the ocean of dreams where he may become one with the wind." Then he released the dead chief's body which floated down river towards the ocean.

The people buried the fallen villagers in the ground to again become one with nature. All the people from every tribe agreed that to stand strong as one nation was the only way to survive. Nikotay had shown he was a great war chief and leader of all native people, friend or foe, and the chiefs and elders agreed that he was the chosen one to lead them.

Pantos walked his daughter over to Nikotay and placed her hand in his. He held his daughter for a moment and then gave them his blessing as he finally realized the great love they had always shared for each other. The young brave looked into Tihla's eyes and she into his. They hugged each other tenderly.

Nikotay then turned to speak to all the people gathered around them. "My brothers and sisters of the earth, I am Nikotay of the great Wolf Clan and I will give my life to protect you. We shall live separately throughout the land, but in our hearts we will always be as one people standing together against those who would come against us. We were the first to be born of Mother Earth and our spirit as a people will always be strong...now and forever...."

THE END

About The Author

Larry "Chas" Silva was born and educated in North Vancouver, British Columbia, as were his mother and father before him. In his heart, he has always been a proud warrior and member of the First Nations communities of North America.

His grandmother, Elizabeth Silva (nee Cordecedo), and his father, Benjamin Silva, were members of the Squamish Nation in North Vancouver. Elizabeth's mother was Katherine Kamonake Tommy and her father and grandfather were hereditary chiefs of their time.

Elizabeth married Silva's grandfather Manuel Silva, a proud Chilean immigrant. Elizabeth's brother, Louis Cordecedo, was a well-known North Vancouverite who once owned some of the land where the Lion's Gate Bridge now stands.

Benjamin Silva married Larry's mother, Joan (nee Palmer), a beautiful Welsh woman in 1947. They had 10 children, of which Larry is the second youngest. Benjamin and grandmother Elizabeth were honored as elders of the Squamish nation.

Silva has two children, Randy Benjamen and Daniel Edward. With his writings, he hopes to give back to First Nations communities as well as inspire younger generations of the world.

Made in the USA
Charleston, SC
02 September 2015